A MAIDEN'S SYMPHONY

PUBLISHED BY

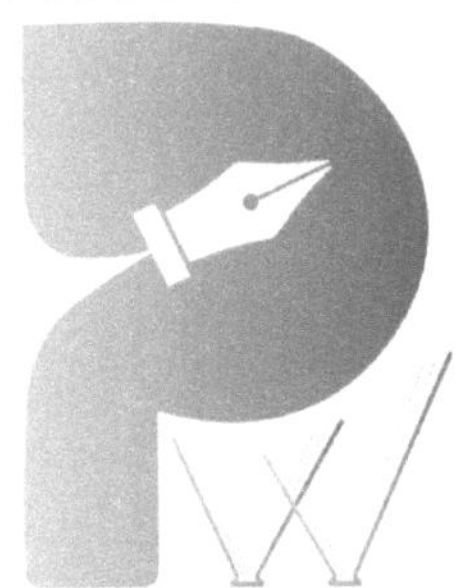

A MAIDEN'S SYMPHONY

AUTHOR

SINJINI CHATTERJEE

<u>Dedication</u>

I want to dedicate this book to

My parents, Rajrupa ma'am (Didibhai), Nabamita ma'am, Biswanath Sir and My brother, Tanu, Sweta.

The people who are always there to encourage,

For whom it happened like a miracle..

With Love,

Sinjini (Mickey)

<u>ABOUT THE BOOK</u>

A Maiden's Symphony is written by an Indian writer, a book bound with collection of poems, short stories micro tales and some inspiring thoughts of the poetess. She pens down the things often unnoticed and overlooked, thoughts and emotions that are often ignored and surpassed. Her pen spins the yarn beautifully into an untold journey and leads us to a realm of beautiful imagination. The trivial joys, emotions and thoughts takes us on a roller coaster ride of life itself.

SINJINI CHATTERJEE

<u>AUTHOR'S BIO</u>

Sinjini Chatterjee is a middle age girl who always dreams for big. She was born and brought up in North Bengal, amidst of nature. She studies Law in Kolkata and aspires to become a lawyer by profession. But apart from that, writing is her passion. She started her writing journey from school days, some of them published in little magazines. she tried her hand on some stand up Open mic in collaboration with YourQuote from where she gathered some impressive response. Her pen flows to express by poems, stories and shayeri. Her writing is her imagination and what she sees through her eyes while others miss out! According to her, when heart bleeds, writing is Solace.

Skiping the part of her bio data she is a fond lover of poetry and novels.Thus she laid down her thoughts and idea into poems, Micro-tales,Short stories. She belives her work would get wings when pieces of her book will touch readers' heart.

As Sinjini says,

"Everyone has a life,
some live, some walk through alive!
as long as words create in you a vibe-
trust me, you can always survive.."

Instagram account- Someday_fr_sure
Facebook Account- Sinjini Chatterjee.

CONTENTS

Seize The Day.. 13

No one's going to know it all........................14

Dear Zindagi...15

The Sunrise..16

Gloomy Window.. 17

Embrace your beliefs................................... 19

The key of memories................................... 20

Let's Live..21

The Lone Traveler... 23

The Last Question.. 24

The Story Book..25

The Alone She... 26

One Day...27

Waves..30

Meet Again..31

The Fake Promise..35

The Forever Love...36

At the end, it matters.................................. 41

A Death So Awaited......................................53

FEEL BEYOND WORDS.................................55

SINJINI CHATTERJEE

POEMS

SINJINI CHATTERJEE

<u>SEIZE THE DAY</u>

Sometimes it happens that days just pass by,
But when you look back,
You feel like for so long cloud didn't meet the sky.
In these hectic days, your words get lost.
And do you think if it's worth the cost?

No, the cost is your time which passes like river,
You have no idea of that flow, you can't buy time
ever.

When you look back, it's just your work,
What about your dreams, that was there?
See, the jar is empty, your wish list in a dustbin.
Have you ever thought, that's how life's going to be?
So, take a while, look forward and think.
Take a pen in your hand and fill the ink.
Then add your dreams to the wish list jar,
It's your dream, it's not going to be far.
Seize the day my friend, live like it's your last day,
Don't ever put your dreams at the bay.
Because, if you do,
One day there will be only regrets and sorrows.
My friend, live your dreams,
As there are very few tomorrows.

<u>NO ONE'S GOING TO KNOW IT ALL</u>

And no one's going to know it all.
No one's going to understand the love you feel for
them.
No one's going to be there to listen one more time,
How much you love them.

Eventually, everyone fades away here.
But they leave the memories for you to bear.
If you were here to leave, then why you came?
Why scratched in my heart, your name?

But you get to understand it's a lonely place to live.
There's nothing more left that you can give.
So, are we still living or surviving?
Close ones packing bags and,
One moment they are just gone.
You're absolutely unworthy, none.
The blank page remains blank,
And no one's going to know it all.

<u>DEAR ZINDAGI</u>

Dear Zindagi,
I know it's been a while.
We didn't even say hi or bye.
But today, I'm here with a thank you note,
It's been a long time even anything I wrote.
Thank you for this beautiful life,
To give a very few people by my side.
Thanks for letting me know quality matters,
Quantities don't.
Thanks for believing I will not quit,
Because, yeah, I won't.
Thanks for giving me mom,
She is the best companion for life,
Thanks for giving me my Guardian Angel,
She is always there by my side.
And of course, a short list of good friends,
Who taught me that friendship never ends.
Thanks for giving me myself,
Today I'm at peace with everything still left.
Thanks for making me believe in forever love,
Even though I know that I can't have.
I'm grateful to you; you're also a friend,
Just stick with me until the very end.
Because, I'm going to rock the world

You'll see,
Just roll with me and whatever happens
Let it be.
Dear Zindagi, for now that's all I can say,
Will be back soon, till then take care, okay?

<u>THE SUNRISE</u>

And after the darkest sleepless nights,
You see the sunrise, like you never did.
The gentle ray touches your skin,
You feel who you are from deep within.

We know, we all are losing everyday,
It's the bitter truth no one says.
But, there are reasons worth living.

There are reasons worth dreaming.
There are reasons to begin once again,
There are reasons for waking up, again.

So before you quit, at your last night,
Take a glance at another sunrise.

<u>GLOOMY WINDOW</u>

And see, this is the irony,
When you look through a gloomy window,
You believe the sun will not burn you.
But when you get outside,
You feel the heat that makes you blow.

Just like this, when we love,
We believe no one's going to hurt us,
But love indeed hurts.
We get messed up, we make life a fuss.
But the same love, makes you believe in forever.
Gives you strength to love over and over.
Just like this, we make disasters in life,
We can't count them one to five.

We shatter people, we make them victim,
But it was us, it was all our crime.
Irony is, it happens like so,
Because,
We see life through a gloomy window,
But to get back, is to love them like you never did.
Just hold their hands so tightly and never ever leave.

Because, that's life all about
We make promises, ones we break,
But there are thousand more vows to take.
You just have to try again and again,

To make them believe in the inner you,
That truly loves the friendship, and them.

So let your mistakes go, let the time flow,
You have another sunrise to try again,
You promised you would love them
Until the very end..

<u>EMBRACE YOUR BELIEFS</u>

And I see the dusk turn to dawn.
We always count what is gone.
And what remained, what is lost,
We count all of the costs,
But there are more if you've seen,
The sun rays which you don't feel,
The gentle wind that embraces you,
The peace which is meant for you.

Look down the road, when the light is low,
You have still a long way yet to go.
Life has never been about big things,
It's the small moments, smile that bring.
Turn those to laughter,
Cherish the memories,
The world is never big enough for
Your beautiful stories.
Live, love, laugh what they always say,
Life is something more, kept in bay.

Don't dim your lights if it's too shiny for others
Because it's your life, don't you ever bother.
Love forever, but don't ever regret,
'Cause hatred never wins life's bet.
It's your choice how you live life,
In every sun rays, embrace your beliefs.

<u>THE KEY OF MEMORIES</u>

And the weather changes,
Like it always did.
The old myself remains in deep,
As it is an old habit.

Yeah, nothing really does change around me,
Nothing makes sense, though meant to be.
Because as you left, you took all with you,
I'm a survivor, like a millions in a queue,
All I know, it's changing,
Except for me.

Because I'm the memories which you made me,
So, memories doesn't change,
Time though flows and goes,
I'm a secret cupboard for years,
The key, lost with you years ago.

<u>LET'S LIVE</u>

And everyday, we question what is life?
May be one question it is, answers are five,
And that's how we keep rolling on,
And like this each day is gone.
What should we do, where to go?
We run for all the answers
And life continues to flow.
We count hatred, we count defeat,
And we forget there is a life to greet.
Aren't we really forgetting something?
Have you a single time, thought about it?

There is love,
There is a thing called blessing,
Look around and see,
Which many are craving,
Yes, it seems too silly what you have,
And thus you and life create a gap.
Wake up, each sunrise says daily,
Carry on, dear heart, though it's heavy,
Because that's the only way to live life,
Look other way round, get positive vibes.
Do whatever you want, follow your passion,
That is your life and you have a vision.
Love yourself, travel your own way.
Don't follow others, they don't have any say,
It's your life, it has always been.

Don't stuck between your 'should and would'
Be different and follow your dreams.
Because, I know life is uncertain
Death is obvious more than this.
Let's breathe freely until you have it.
Because, dear heart if you trust me,
With the moments,
Life will always continue to flow,
Make your own tale with memories,
As there is nothing called tomorrow.

<u>THE LONE TRAVELER</u>

You and I both travelled a lot,
The roads which hadn't even crossed,
The journey was yet unnamed,
To you, of course it was a shame,
But as for me,
I don't have something to say,
Love always kept me at the bay.
Yet the hope echoes still now,
To ask me again, I'm doing it how?
Because you stopped there, I didn't.
You had a choice,
My love gave you freedom.
I'm a loner, of course I'm.
But to me,
Love doesn't lose its charm.
Every single day I just try,
I know I'm born to fly.
I'll be a wanderer,
I'll always be.
But the stars will watch me,
They will make you see,
That love is forever,
To me it is always just,
I just have to follow the stars and,
Love is my compass.

<u>THE LAST QUESTION</u>

And then she asked,
'Why do you still love me?
Even with all my scars?'
He stopped, took a breath,
'I love you, I do, because
The sky never leaves the stars'
'Why do you come to me, why?
After all the things I did to you,
Why you never left, not for a day,
Isn't my story scary?'
He paused, taking her hand into his,
He whispered,
'The thing between you and me is,
Just Gravity'

<u>THE STORY BOOK</u>

And every now and then,
I look up to the vast sky.
May be in search of memories,
But then I just see time to fly,
What remained, what is lost,
What I wanted at every cost,
But you walked on so fast,
You've never been slow
I denied to run for love, but
Never wanted to let you go.
As you would turn the pages and
Live happily rest of the life,
You would never hear
Someone wrote a whole book
For you, with all silent tears,
Which would be turned to ashes,
When he would've died.

<u>THE ALONE SHE</u>

It looks harder to fall down
Seven times, stand up eight
It asks more a warrior, less
a girl who burns so bright.
May be the time was wrong,
May be most stubborn was she
But nobody could ever let her down,
She was always, who she wanted to be.

Some showed her how painful it is,
To be a girl, and have a life to live,
Whereas some faces reminded her,
There is so much in the world to give.

Now that she came a long way
Daring not to wear even a mask,
She knows how beautiful it is,
To be you, even the hardest task.

Now that all are in peace, as she is
She craves for a face in the crowd
A hand to hold her hand as it is.
Not all of them know,
She also doesn't want to show,
The heart that she kept deep down,
Waiting, still for a prince with a crown.

<u>ONE DAY</u>

One day, I'll meet you again,
In the same place,
In a perplexed state;
When you'd look at me,
And without a smile,
You'd say, "Hey!"

Memories would flash by,
As you'd stare,
Into my eye,
To find that emotion,
Which once,
Had the name of care.

With nothing found,
No love and no hatred
Profound,
You'd look away,
And say,
"Good to see you around."

My eyes would question,
Your existence
And mine,
Recall that moment,
When I was,
Meant to be thine.

"Let it go," you'd say,
As I'd look up,
To meet your gaze,
Wondering,
If you were the one,
For whom I had been suffering all along.

Without an answer,
I'd look away;
'Cause you would never be,
The one, who'd stay.

As I'd walk ahead,
You'd want,
To stop me,
To hold me still,
And to shake me enough,
And to talk to me.

But you wouldn't
Make that effort,
As you'd know,
The reason for which,
I would have walked back,
Without a word.

And as I'd walk ahead,
I'd silently pray,
That never in your life,
Would you ever leave,
Another girl, abandoned,
In any way.

Because, one day,
I'll meet you again,
In the same place,
In a perplexed state;
When you'd look at me,
And without a smile,
Would say, "Hey!"

<u>WAVES</u>

Who do the waves belong to?
The sea or the shore?
Many say the sea
And true that may be.

Except,

Why do the waves reach out for the shore?
Day and night, night and day
Since time began?

Just to cast a loving caress upon the shore
Then be gone again?

I say the waves are like me
Fighting off fear and uncertainity
Leaving behind all familiarity
Just to touch the shore one more time,
Each time.

In the hope that one day
You will reach out to touch me as well
Then catch me and never let me go
So we can finally be together,
Forever.

<u>MEET AGAIN</u>

Now that you're far away, you are gone
I'm left like abandoned, just left to moan,
I really don't do that, I watch time to fly,
I know our love's alive, just as stars for sky.
I know it's hard to love, it also leaves scars
Sky even fails to hold on, shooting us stars,
But as they always say,
True love never dies in vain,
I know, I believe, I hope,
We will meet again,
We will meet again.

SINJINI CHATTERJEE

MICRO-TALES

SINJINI CHATTERJEE

THE FAKE PROMISE

They met after ten years in School Reunion.

They, 'Once the Best Friend Couple', everyone adored.

He, a successful Writer and she with her husband, may be the richest.

After quite a few time, the ice broke. She came over and said, 'So your dream came true. Passion, Fame..You have everything.'

He smiled quietly and started to walk. And then suddenly he turned around and said, 'Actually, I don't have one thing that you have.'

'What?,' she asked smiling.

'Regret! You left me for your dominant boyfriend, now husband and others once. I never did. So, you're a winner buddy'

Then he walked away and shedding a tear he whispered, 'And you promised me a forever even if It's hell, Irony'

And she was standing there like she could ever move, sobbing.

Some stories are yet a mystery.

<u>THE FOREVER LOVE</u>

And at the Silver Jubilee of School they met. The childhood lovers, once they were. He entered and looked at her, the same smile, the same pretty look and gorgeous she was, wearing a saree.

He knew she became a scientist; her dream came true though it always felt like his. Suddenly, she looked back and there was one glance between them, like before. An awkward silence was revolving in the chaos.

A few minutes passed by, seemed like a decade. Lost in her thoughts, everything was fading away.

'I read all of your books,' the same voice he was dying to hear every day.

Quietly, he said, 'And that never made you remember me?'

'Nope,' she said, 'Because I was always in them.'

He smiled. 'Why didn't you ever stop loving me, even after all these years?,' she said.

'That's the only thing I can't do, I promised you forever' and he turned around to hide his tear.

'Will you not drop me home? Like always?' she asked, her voice choking.

He didn't ask anything, 'Just drive then,' he said.

'Let's walk,' she said with the smile that was only for him..

And that night, full of stars, they walked and lived every moment. Before leaving, she kissed him on his cheek like school days.

May be that's what love is. You can't define it ever in life.

SHORT STORIES

SINJINI CHATTERJEE

AT THE END, IT MATTERS

1ˢᵗ October, 2020

After everyone left, Rayan sat in the airport, quietly. He looked at the offer letter from the Newcastle University, UK, his passport and visa. He laughed at himself sarcastically and said, "So, Rayan Chatterjee, ultimately you're leaving. Have you ever thought it would be your destiny, even five years ago? Or was it destined to be? You're not leaving Rayan, you're escaping. This commonwealth scholarship, this letter, all of these are a part of your drama. And the only person, who knows about it, is your maa, who just left with silent tears a few minutes ago. Okay, let's play this game as the way you wanted. Or should I say, the way she wanted it to be?"

The last call for the flight broke Rayan's illusion. Carrying his handbag, he left, drowning all his dreams, smiles and the real Rayan who was alive once upon a time. He just left silently.

Five years ago,

Everyone thinks that "School life love" is a myth. But Debapriya and Rayan never ever thought about it. From class ten to the end of class twelve today, they defined their relationship in their own way. Like every other day, when the tuition ended, Rayan came closer and held his Priya's hands so tightly. They both knew, after the exams, their colleges would be different; there will be a long distance relationship. But they knew, their love is enough to cover all these things. They love each other so much.

"Let's put an end to it," Priya broke the silence suddenly and left Rayan's hand.

"What? You're joking right? Come on, give me a hug," Rayan said smilingly.

"Don't take it as a joke Ray, we discussed it previously also. My family will never ever accept any relationship. You know that very well. It's better to end it now. We can't even spend a day apart from each other now. The more years, the more pain it would cost."

Rayan came closer to Priya, "We talked about it, right? We have time. Both of us will get a job and apart from that, my family business is there. Everything will be sorted. Just give it some time. Be calm, be us, okay? I'm not leaving you."

"Time will not change the conservative mind-set of my mother Ray! Do you want me to leave my family? That's what you want?" Priya was full of anger, at least pretending to be.

"I never wanted that Priya, you know me. We are family friends and I always treated your family as mine too," Rayan said so calmly.

"Then don't waste time with words. Just end it now. Otherwise, I'll be in pain for you, but there is nothing I can do about it," a cold voice came out, which Rayan never heard or was never known of.

"But what about me? Almost four years we are together, I'll be lost, I'll be.." before Rayan could finish, Priya stopped him, "Nothing would happen. One day you will forget everything and me too! Just go! Go somewhere where I could never find you, go!"

After few minutes, Rayan turned back and started to walk away, his head bent down. He started to walk away from all those hugs and kisses, all those crazy fights, all those promises which were meant to be true. And behind, a girl was standing in silence, teary eyed. She only saw her sunshine, her Ray walking away, walking away with love. Their forever love!

After shock, after the exams, Priya only came for one day in excuse of taking books. In spite of that, she took all of Rayan's poems, stories and paintings. She always wanted Rayan to be a writer. Before leaving, she kissed Rayan on his lips so hard and kissed his forehead with so much affection, "That's the only thing I can have. I can have for lifetime! It's a good bye Ray," she whispered and left, without turning back. Rayan was a patient of depression since then. For six months, he had gone through several therapies, sedatives etc. He did not know what to do with life, career! He just recalled their dreams. Priya and Rayan wanted to open an

NGO, Priya loves trees and Rayan loves animals. They wanted to create a small planet for those where they can breathe freely. Along with that an orphanage and a school for those kids, where they will teach and live together for a lifetime. But if all we wish becomes true, then there would never have been difference between dreams and reality.

So, after six months, Rayan found himself in a University to study BA-LLB (H), Law. Priya always wanted him to be a writer. The first day when Rayan was at the gate of the University, he whispered to himself-

"When my mind is so chaotic,
Just so blurry as am I,
When I'm tired of all these
When I need a shoulder to cry.
I reach out to you, I do.
May be the voice remains silent,
May be your phone doesn't ring,
May be a message undelivered
You don't even want to see.
I reach out to you silently,
I talk with you in my head,
And that 'you' gives me peace
The only awaited bed rest.
I know, we are strangers now,
You don't know what I am facing
But you're the only name I know,
Your hands that I'm craving.

Because, I never knew a name,
I never knew how to share pain.
It's you, who held me for so long,
All I ever had is you, now not here.
But still, all I know is your name,
You'll be always my forever."

This is my last poem Priya, Rayan smiled after finishing. Ray is no more." And then, Rayan took his first step to the University.

Surprisingly, Rayan's life changed after taking this course. The only way to live is to work, that Rayan found. Rayan keep scoring high in each semester, making his family proud. Only in vacation, Rayan used to see a face who knows the truth, Maa.

One day Maa asked Rayan, "For how long are you going to punish yourself and me? I want my son back."

"I'm right here Mamma, chill," Rayan faked a smile. After some moments, both of them shed their tears silently.

Actually, Rayan never wanted to be a topper or apple of everyone's eyes. He was trying hard to find a loop hole, to run away. Because, even with sedatives, sleep was a luxury.

All that Rayan could hear, "Go away!" and by all means, Rayan had to keep his promise. When someone works so hard, opportunities come along.

In the fourth year of his course, Rayan was able to take International Law as his Hons. Paper. And from that point, he started to find out how to go to abroad for higher studies. The process was not as easy as it sounded. There were a lot of agencies to fool everyone and studying abroad on his own was a farfetched dream. But Rayan did not stop hunting for one opportunity.

Meanwhile, a message came in Rayan's phone, "I am now a junior research fellow at Tata Institute of Fundamental Research Centre. I had to share the big news, right? So do you, hopefully very soon.-Debapriya." Rayan smiled, tears in his eyes, both of happiness and broken heart.

A voice came from underneath, "You can never be Debapriya to me Priya. You'll always be my Priya. Congratulations."

After this, Rayan realized he cannot stay here anymore. He cannot stay apart from Priya being in same country, same hometown. He had to do something. Weeks went, months too. Finally Rayan found the place, the right place to approach.

He took a shot to apply for Commonwealth Scholarship. He knew it was not going to be easy. Because, knowledge matters more than your grades. The preliminary round was held in Ministry of Human Resource Development (MHRD). The day Rayan booked his flight; maa came closer and said, "You will never find solace by escaping. You are just taking my son away and also the person who is so loved by his friends and teachers for a kind heart. Go, find yourself if you can." Rayan had no answer and no more tears were left.

He became stone hearted. He was becoming selfish just to keep promises. But deep down, he knew, one day he would do something which would make Maa proud. The preliminary round went well. Simultaneously, his exams were going on too. All Rayan understood was, he became a pressure cooker.

Few months later, a mail came to Rayan's mailbox. Yeah, he was shortlisted! But was he happy or sad? No feelings popped up in his heart. All he knew was, he had to go for it. The interview panel made Rayan shiver from inside. It was not only about law. It was about everything! His perspective, his ambition, his life goals etc. etc. All Rayan gave were fake answers except one. The answer was, he wants to come back and do job for the nation, build a NGO by taking baby steps.

After that it was like an indefinite time to wait. Most importantly, Rayan had to get a good grade and his degree to crack this one, he knew. He was drowning into work and finally he got gold medal in his degree. Alongside, he achieved the dream which was just an illusion even five years ago. And after achieving all these, Rayan just felt empty and blank! He had nothing to say or do. He just felt, five years passed away without you Priya! How many years it would take for a lifetime? Actually, each and every day without your loved one costs you a lifetime! For these five years, Rayan felt it every second.

But now, there is no turning back. It is the high time for Rayan to fly. Before leaving, there were twenty days left for Rayan to spend at his hometown. He spent every minute with Maa and his brother, the two people who loved him the most. Before the day of leaving, Rayan opened his phone and started typing....

"Going far away where you could never find me. I hope you will be happy with your family and from core of my heart, I wish you success in every aspect of life. Still, with love - Ray."

Within a moment, the phone popped up, "Will you never come back?"

"Obviously! Our dream is mine now. And I have to make it happen. Just few years it is! If possible, come to me then, when all your responsibilities would be over. Till then, take care."

"Now it is a good bye Ray. Just remember, you are mine. You will always be mine. Promise me."

"That's a forever promise Priya. I can only be yours. Without you, I can't be myself ever. That's a promise. Good bye."

20 years later, Present Day

Eventually, Rayan loved to live in foreign and travel. His first dream was not a dream, it was an escaping plan. But, when he grew up, he understood that the dream anyone is passionate about has to be true. To make a dream come true, you have to work so hard! Rayan became a blog writer in the domain of law and also in many other aspects.

He became a motivational speaker too, irony! From a depressed boy to a motivation, the journey was like a roller-coaster ride. But he made another promise too. So, five years ago, Rayan flew back to India, his motherland. Building an NGO on his own was the most difficult job in these twenty years. Rayan was not happy, but after he made that, he is at peace now.

Only one thing shattered him in the past. One day maa called and let him know about Priya's wedding. Since then, she is Debapriya Sen. It took time, a lot of time to heal himself. But one day Rayan realized, after everything is gone, what remains, that is counted as love. He was so loved, all these years; Priya's memories furnished him with love!

Today, he made a front page in a magazine. According to them, his NGO, "TITLI" is a touch of green earth in this concrete world. He made it but it can never be complete without Priya and it won't be. Quietly, Rayan was sitting in his room. A room, filled with vintage pictures of him and Priya, her favourite books, their letters, their favourite songs.

In short, this is Rayan's whole world. He was sipping coffee, suddenly a voice came, "I am home." A voice which Rayan craved to hear for last twenty years. His coffee mug slipped as he turned back and saw Priya standing in front of him. The same face, the same smile, the same orchid smell made Rayan stunned. Priya was also standing and Rayan couldn't understand why was she smiling so much?

The ice broke after few moments, "Debapriya Sen is here!" Rayan said. Suddenly. Priya dropped her bags and came closer to Rayan and gave him a tight slap! Rayan didn't not know what to say and what is happening!

"Only Priya is here, you understand? And that will be Priya Chatterjee tomorrow, mark my words!" Priya was hissing while saying those words.

"What do you mean? I am not getting you! You are not supposed to be here now. You have a family."

"Who said me to come over when my responsibilities are over? Yes Rayan, I got married. After all society and family take away what you want. But I got my divorce after six months when my mother passed away. I was independent; I worked all those years and searched for you everywhere. But, for your information, the world is not a tiny place. Thanks to this magazine otherwise I would have never found you. And if my surname bothers you so much, tear all these pictures and I'll be gone too, I promise," Priya said all these in a rush, she could not breathe.

Slowly, Rayan came closer to Priya, "For me, you are always Priya Chatterjee. And your surname can't be greater than your love..I love you Priya.."

"Can you hug me Ray? Can you hug me tightly like before?" Priya was sobbing.

Rayan hugged Priya like he would never let her go, he doesn't know for how much time! Then he kissed Priya gently and said, "Everything is same Priya, there is no before or after. I am forever yours, remember?"

"So?" Priya put her head on Rayan's chest. "So..", Rayan said, "We made a journey of forever love together. At the end, it mattered. It matters.." Priya kissed Rayan gently and they held their hands together and walked together whole day in their planet, TITLI. And priya started to recite one of Rayan's poems -

"And thus I try to find a never land,
A place where I see you and me to stand..
And I imagine how it would be,

How you would just talk or hug me!
I try to know whether there would be solace,
Just you and I, and words will run flawless!
I would kiss you like a shy lover,
And you'll promise me again our forever.
We'll hold hands and walk around,
We'll be gone and never wanted to be found!
And a deep forest and fire would be lit,
And the stars will also see the long awaited kiss.
I'll wait for the day like a lone island,
My love, there will be our never land.."

And thus their love story met its destiny. A love story which travelled for long 20 years.

<u>A DEATH SO AWAITED</u>

One Side of the Mirror:-

There she is, my love, so close to me, Aarov saw and just ran towards her. All the bars behind him became blurred. After lifetime he awaited, he hugged her and kissed like never before. She smiled back and held his hands tightly, and took him home. Oh! Peace.. Then Aarov felt like falling asleep, on her lap..

The Other Side:-

"It's unfortunate", the Senior doctor of the Asylum said to the new intern, "He was a patient of insomnia, panic attacks. He was hallucinating for a year but he never behaved like an insane."

"How did all this happen? He used to behave with me normally! He always used to make up stories," the intern girl shed tears.

"Oh! It's the same old story ever, 'love'!" the doctor sighed, "He had a relationship with a girl for 5 years and then she left, they belonged to different castes!"

"That's why, that's why. He always mentioned a girl, the same girl every time!" the intern screamed.

"Oh, don't be so excited, it happens here!" The doctor continued, "And everyone hasn't got the same nerve to handle it, he couldn't. After two years he got admitted here, when the girl got married. But he was okay. He was becoming calmer day by day."

"But then? How did he..?"

"Excuse me lady, doctors don't have all the answers, have they? It's love and it is always undefined!" He paused for a second and took a deep breath, "He was perfectly fit today and it seems like, what to say, the kiss of death! Inform his family, he is no more. God granted him forever sleep!"

The doctor stood up and left quietly. And after so many years, Aarov slept peacefully. At last, freedom was given in name of death.

FEEL BEYOND WORDS

WHY IT'S YOU?

Someday soon, you're going to sit in a crowded room, a room full of people eager to listen to you! Just like now you're staring at the mirror hopelessly! Someday soon, people are going to find the meaning of hope from your own tale and will head back to home, to start again the next day!

Someday very soon, you will be known as an inspiration, may be not to billions but thousands of people. Doesn't it matter? If it does, then don't look around hopelessly all the time! Don't ask any question to your mirror image, "Why me?"

Just give a glance of determination and say, 'yeah, try me!'

Because, someday very soon, you both are going to smile looking at each other, before entering a room, full of people, waiting for you with a huge round of applause!

And only because of that, it's you, it has to be you. Because, believe, you are a winner not a Survivor.

Let's hope and believe in yourself!

COMPANION FOR LIFE

Did you ever sit in dark with teary eyes, not weeping as too tired to cry and someone just sat beside you? Neither she consoled, nor gave any advice, just made you feel, 'yes, I'm there'

Have you ever, just slipped while walking on the road, may be on the path of life also and someone just held your hand tightly, made you stand up?

When there was a time, you achieved something great, and someone's cheers and shouting over shadowed your happiness? And more than that achievement, those cheers made you more grateful?

Did it happen with you, you shouted and fight with that person several times and those days without her made you feel miserable! And then a smile between you two sorted it all, without even a sorry?

And then we want to term it with huge names and all that, but you know what this is? This is friendship. I don't know about the tags, 'Best friend, Bestest friend' and all that. I just know friendship itself is very special.

While sometimes, love breaks you into pieces, a friend even loves the pieces and makes a masterpiece.

I have one in my life, just one. Apart from all the tags, a companion for my life. I believe so. And I will always cling to her no matter what. She has to be there.

So, if you also got someone in your life just like that, irritate them, fight with them, hug them tightly and last but not the least, love them.. There is nothing beautiful than a true friendship, trust me, nothing.

<u>YOUR STORY ISN'T OVER</u>

You know over the years, I realized our pain can't be compared to others. Because, we all go through different situations. The only thing we have in common is 'Pain'. But there's no reason to hide it from all. Because, it is an inevitable part of our lives.

We all see our close people dying in front of our eyes, we see our relationships get broken, we all get ditched by friends whom we count on the most! And there are many other things also!

We need sleeping pills, anti depressants, we get drunk and do more dumb things and that's absolutely fine. You can't avoid pain, just like happiness. We want happiness all the time but truth is, these two are vice versa. Without one of them, you can't value the other one. There's nothing to be ashamed of, it's okay. Life gives us lessons in these ways.

But my point is, you don't need to pretend as the strongest person when you're vulnerable. You don't need to be the lion of the forest! Rather than that, be the phoenix of your life, rise from the ashes over and over again.

It's okay to fall down a hundred times until you get up and face the world again. Because, this is not your story, this is not meant to be. Don't ask yourself every time, 'Why me?'

Have the courage to get back to life. Failure can always be a part, but giving up can never be.

At the high time of giving up, turn back to life again. In every sun rays, embrace your believes. Because, at the end of the day you're the gem of your life.

Cling to life, only.

<u>PLACES, MEMORIES AND MY HEART</u>

I find it crazy, how people turn their way back from you, so soon! One fine day, you two are walking on the same road and the other day, that person has already chosen another way! It's just the worst feeling you can ever have! I've learnt in my short life span, that people are never ready for a good bye. Yes, they truly aren't. No matter how much aware they are, it still hurts the same. And a surprise good bye? Cost your whole life!

But the places, damn, the places always remain the same. Years go on and you can still get the familiar smell whenever you come across! And of course, a flash back is a free curse added with that. And the hardest part, that you never know whether it's a gift or curse! Because, while people move on, places remind us of what we were, at some point of time, together. It was a fairy tale!

But then also, fairy tales have an end! And life goes on. we come back, turn around from the places and our wounds, unable to heal and we carry on. With a hope that someday, we would be back again to the same places, where we left our hearts to live peacefully.

Or maybe, one day when I would be standing in one of the places, you would turn around, to me, to our memories. You will heal me and maybe we would start all over again, maybe.

<u>A MORNING NOTE</u>

As usual, after a long, dark night, the sun rises as an old habit. There is nothing new about it, especially when you are going through a rough phase. A morning seems to be another tiring day for you. The morning reminds you that at some point of life, we are all alone. There might be a lot of people around you but they will hardly give you their hand to overcome the day. They have their own lives, their own battles. This will again make you remember; someday you had your life too! With a beautiful person in it! You would have no idea of your thinking process! It works like so.

Sometimes it is more pathetic to open your eyes at morning than to be awake. You can turn back your face from the world even when you are awake, because no one knows. But as soon as you open your eyes, you have to face the world. There is no other option left.

Holding this thought, I woke up today, with no energy left! But then I made an imaginary call to my love, we did talk about childhood days, memories and it included that person only. Because, she was and always will be an inseparable part of my life. And it was strange that I feel so good talking about those days! It's completely crazy that for whom you are depressed, talking about that person can make you feel better!

Then I realized what it is all about. Whenever we miss a person, we miss memories the most.

May be we have grown apart, but as long as memories are there, we are connected with that person. Love is something that always leaves its marks, called memories. Keep them; cherish them, as long as you can. While everything fades away, memories keep their place safe in our hearts, so do love-if it's true.

From that moment, I cherished the feeling as much I can. I know it's a while where I'm feeling okay, and it will be gone soon. Because pain is inevitable, you can't resist, you can't deny. You just have to walk along with it, unless it becomes your habit.

But I can promise you that you can live. I can say that because I also have gone through it, and going through. It's a journey you have to complete. But as long as memories are there, you will always find love. You just have to learn to love yourself too. And one day, these all will be worth it.

<u>DEEP INSIDE</u>

If you ever bump into her, tell her that I'm happy and yes, I'm living my own life. Tell her about my career, how I'm doing completely well. Tell her about my achievements so far and my future goals. Tell her my success story, my ambitions and my completely settled life.

If you see her, make sure you don't let her get a whiff of that I still think of her every night before sleeping. Don't tell her that she is still in my head and I spend all the 'Only me' time with her memories. Don't tell her that I still wish that whenever I have a bad dream I can call her up without any second thought. Don't tell her I miss our late night talks, where we discussed everything from work to studies to dreams. If you meet her, make sure you talk about me, my survival. But don't let her know how much I crave for her warm hug during those struggles!

If you meet her, tell her that I'm done away with all her gifts that she gave me, but don't let her know they are all remaining in my favorite corner of cupboard. Don't tell her I still read the letters she gave me and cry myself to sleep on the days I miss her most, almost every day! Don't tell her that I miss seeing her name in my chat heads and my call logs. And the emptiness I feel, I want to forget with our call recordings.

If you see her, talk about my professional achievements but make sure you don't bring up my personal life, because she'll get to know, 'I'm barely living.' Don't let her know that with every shooting star, I just wish to hold her hand one last time, hug her one last time. Don't tell her I don't eat black forest pastry anymore because it reminds me of her. If you see her, tell her only half the truth.

If you see her, tell her I wish her the best of luck in every aspect of life. But make sure she doesn't know if she ever wants to come back, I will let her back into my life, in a single heart beat..!

MIDNIGHT THOUGHTS

There was a time in my life, when all the nights were full of smile, laughter. I remember I used to tell someone stories and she always fell asleep in midst of it. We used to talk about dreams, our future goals, silly things and day after tomorrow. There was a time, when every night we talked about when we're going to meet the next time, because at that time, we stored our daily gossips to share at the next meeting. I think, most of the time she did so, I loved to listen and smile only. We used to fight at night some days and the very next morning, a 'Good Morning' text solved it all.

There was a time, when a night was incomplete without her good night. There was a time; I slept in peace, without worries and stress. Because I knew, no matter what happens, she will be there to hold me. Night does come now, with darkness, with fear and it makes me restless. I do sleep now with 8 sleeping pills, but sometimes I wake up shaken. I never dream now, all are only nightmares. I fear, I shiver from inside. Because I know, now you are not there to hold my hands anymore.

At that time in nights, we made plans to travel, to cook, to do shopping and to have lots of fun. There was a 'To-Do list', our wish list! Trust me; I didn't visit those places we promised to go together, because somewhere I hope we would do these together.

Nowadays, I even don't know if we would see us again or not. Whenever I see a dream, it's all about you. I smile in my dream, and feel choked when I get up, realizing it as a dream..

With every night-end, the count of my sighs increases. Because, 'We' are now too far-fetched from reality! But with every new dawn, I keep a hope that, we'll meet again. Somewhere, someday. I'll keep waiting.

<u>DESERVED</u>

I'm at a point now, where I feel whatever I've got, I completely deserved. May be some grievances killing me inside. No one forced me to feel so, but I'm having this thought. Some voices, some visuals flashing in front of my eyes. Sometimes, when I used to get angry, some moments when I didn't even look back to see what she was feeling, and she continued to say 'Sorry'. It is only my fault, I feel these days.

There was a point in life, where I should have understood she is the most special person I got. She was the only one who loved me more than enough and I didn't even say a thanks! There were some moments in my life, where I should have told her, yes I love you so much and you mean a lot to me. I never did! She wasn't taken for granted. Though I knew, I never expressed.

I thought, I would get a lot of time to say all these, and this is where I made the biggest mistake. There is nothing called TIME, what we feel, we must say at that moment only. The world is a huge place and people disappear in a blink of our eyes. We remain stuck in between our 'Should and would".

Now that she is gone, I don't count her mistakes or mine. All I feel, I should have said all these, before she left. Now that she is not here, I feel her presence the most. May be people come closer to you by leaving you. Whenever I close my eyes, I see her. And I hopelessly wish if I get a chance to say her all in my heart. And as there's no way left, I know what happened, I truly deserved.

<u>SOMETIMES AND FEELINGS</u>

Sometimes, I don't know what I go through. At the hit of the moment, I just feel down. Before that, everything was more than fine, you laugh, and you smile. Deep inside I Know, I'm not a happy soul but I don't want myself to be down. I want to make people happy, I want them to be cheered up, I want to do all the stuffs for my friends. May be, deep within, I'm not counted to be anyone's friend. May be, that's how life goes on.

I don't know why silly things bother me, like my little best friend growing up, like my forever companion leaving for just like 3 days! May be, nowadays, I just feel scared to be alone. I mean, I've been alone before. Like for months, years, that passed on. And now a few days scare me? Who am I? An eight year old kid? I've seen the worse days that I don't even wish for my enemies. I have seen people die in front of my eyes, I saw my love go away.. I have been a loner for years. So what now? Is it depression that's attacking me again?

Seriously, I don't want anyone to bother, especially Maa.. May be that's what my life destined to be. A lonely road lies ahead, a long way to go. May be, the road would be slippery, sometimes filled with snow. But that's how my life always has been. I have to walk through it, carrying warmth in my heart, that may be on my last day, I'll be able to see the sunshine that I wanted for my whole life..!

<u>WHERE DO I BELONG?</u>

The question I guess crossed your mind at some point of life. You thought about it or not, you intended or not, it surely did. And this question tore the strength you hold completely! Because where you belong is what you are!

It was just a chilly morning today and this question came into my mind while walking towards the highway, in midst of hundred more people. And the very next moment, I was blank! I think, life is a journey of moving from one question to another. The reply you really won't get, all you find will, the phases, the path you will walk through, the lessons you will learn, the experiences you will gather.

Today, I really don't know where I belong. All I know I have lost somewhere completely, again. I really have no idea what to do now. My heart says to let go and to hold on. I don't know what it really says, because I think I'm running away from the message of my heart. I just felt, I would not have whom I want the most and tragedy is, knowing and accepting are two different things!

It leaves you nowhere. It stabs you, it hurts. But we just cling to it, as it is love. I live for people around me, to see the smile on their faces but in midst all of these, I don't get to find me. I'm happy I believe, I try to heal others. But the darkness remains inside me only. I can't quit for others, I can't run away! But the 'Me' inside myself is fading away..

Where I belong, they feel with them I do. But I'm far far away! Whenever I close my eyes, I see a face, I see us smiling together, I see some moments shining from a distance. Is this the place I belong? Is it there? Is it you and me? Or it is just another life, where I have never been?

Where I do belong?, I ask me, repeatedly, hopelessly. And I see a tunnel in my head! I see, I'm going inside, taking the steps, a dark big tunnel..

May be someday, the tunnel would take a turn and my eyes will sparkle in sunlight. May be then, I will find where I really do belong..!

9 789389 959147